Dear Parents,

Welcome to the Scholastic Reader series. We have taken over 80 years of experience with teachers, parents, and children and put it into a program that is designed to match your child's interests and skills.

Level 1—Short sentences and stories made up of words kids can sound out using their phonics skills and words that are important to remember.

Level 2—Longer sentences and stories with words kids need to know and new "big" words that they will want to know.

Level 3—From sentences to paragraphs to longer stories, these books have large "chunks" of texts and are made up of a rich vocabulary.

Level 4—First chapter books with more words and fewer pictures.

It is important that children learn to read well enough to succeed in school and beyond. Here are ideas for reading this book with your child:

- Look at the book together. Encourage your child to read the title and make a prediction about the story.
- Read the book together. Encourage your child to sound out words when appropriate. When your child struggles, you can help by providing the word.
- Encourage your child to retell the story. This is a great way to check for comprehension.
- Have your child take the fluency test on the last page to check progress.

Scholastic Readers are designed to support your child's efforts to learn how to read at every age and every stage. Enjoy helping your child learn to read and love to read.

—**Francie Alexander**
Chief Education Officer
Scholastic Education

For my fourth-grade friend, Gayle
—K.M.

To "Biff" Heins
—M.S.

Text copyright © 1999 by Kate McMullan.
Illustrations copyright © 1999 by Mavis Smith.
Activities copyright © 2003 Scholastic Inc.
All rights reserved. Published by Scholastic Inc.
SCHOLASTIC, CARTWHEEL BOOKS, FLUFFY THE CLASSROOM GUINEA PIG,
and associated logos are trademarks and/or registered trademarks of Scholastic Inc.

Library of Congress Cataloging-in-Publication Data is available.

ISBN: 0-590-52310-4

10 9 8 7 6 5 4   05 06 07
Printed in the U.S.A. 23 • First printing, March 1999

FLUFFY
MEETS THE DINOSAURS

by **Kate McMullan**

Illustrated by **Mavis Smith**

Scholastic Reader — Level 3

SCHOLASTIC INC.

New York   Toronto   London   Auckland   Sydney
Mexico City   New Delhi   Hong Kong   Buenos Aires

Fluffy Rules!

Wade and Maxwell put Fluffy
in his play yard.
They put in lots of toy dinosaurs, too.
"Fluffy meets the dinosaurs!" said Wade.
Hey, dinosaurs, thought Fluffy.

"It is the age of the dinosaurs," said Wade.

"Dinosaurs rule the earth."

Those little things? thought Fluffy.

"Dinosaurs are fierce," said Maxwell.

"They are very, very powerful."

You must be joking, thought Fluffy.

Wade picked up a long dinosaur.

He stomped it around.

"I am thunder lizard!" he roared.

In your dreams, thought Fluffy.

Maxwell picked up a big-headed dinosaur.

He stomped it around.

"I am king of the dinosaurs!" he growled.

"T-rex rules!"

I don't think so, thought Fluffy.

Maxwell made T-rex bite Wade's dinosaur.

Wade made his dinosaur roar.

The two dinosaurs began to fight.

Wade and Maxwell made strange
dinosaur noises with their mouths.

Soon more dinosaurs joined the battle.

Hey, watch the food dish! thought Fluffy.

You're messing up my play yard!

But the dinosaurs kept fighting.

"Math time!" called Ms. Day.

Wade and Maxwell put the dinosaurs down.

They went back to their seats.

Fluffy was alone with the dinosaurs.

Fluffy began running around his yard.

He kick-boxed the thunder lizard.

He took a flying leap
and stomped on T-rex.
He kept kicking and stomping.
Soon, not a dinosaur was left standing.

The age of dinosaurs is over,
Fluffy thought.
Now it is the age of guinea pigs.
Fluffy rules!

Fluffy's Great Adventure

"Today is our field trip
to the Natural History Museum,"
Ms. Day told her class.
"Did everyone bring a bag lunch?"
All the kids held up their lunch bags.

Wade put his lunch bag down.

He picked up Fluffy.

"We are going to a dinosaur museum!"

Wade told Fluffy.

Why not a Fluffy museum? thought Fluffy

"Too bad you can't come," said Wade.

Who says I can't? thought Fluffy.

And when Wade put him down for a second,
Fluffy crawled into Wade's lunch bag.

Ms. Day's class rode a bus to the museum.

Everyone sat in a courtyard to eat lunch.

Wade opened his lunch bag
and took out his sandwich.

"Yuck!" he said.

Fluffy poked his head out of the bag.

Yuck? thought Fluffy. **It was yummy!**

"Yikes!" said Wade when he saw Fluffy.

"Ms. Day!" he called. "Look who's here!"

"Fluffy!" exclaimed Ms. Day.

"How did you ever get into that bag?"

I'll never tell, thought Fluffy.

"Our class pet Fluffy came with us,"
Wade told the museum guide.
The guide took Fluffy from Wade.
"What a pretty little cavy," he said.
Hey, watch your mouth! thought Fluffy.

"*Cavy* is the scientific name
for guinea pig," the guide explained.
"Let's go inside.
I'll show you Fluffy's cousins.
I'll show you his ancestors, which are
his great, great, great, great, great,
great, great, great, great grandparents."

Ms. Day's class followed the guide
into the museum.
They stopped by a glass case.
A sign on the case said RODENTS.
"Rodents are animals that like to gnaw,"
the guide said.
"They have very sharp front teeth.
Fluffy is a member of the rodent family."
Cool, thought Fluffy.

"Mice are rodents, too," the guide said.
"That means mice are Fluffy's cousins."
No way! thought Fluffy.
"So are rats," added the guide.
No, no, no! thought Fluffy.

Fluffy growled.

But the guide did not seem to notice.

He only walked to the next glass case.

"These are Fluffy's ancestors," he said.

"They came from South America.

They are called wild cavies."

Wild! thought Fluffy. **That's me!**

"Wild cavies were plump," the guide said.
"Bigger animals liked to eat them."
Hold it right there! thought Fluffy.

"Only cavies that hid did not get eaten,"
the guide went on. "They survived."
Fluffy looked into the case.
He saw two small furry animals hiding
in the tall grass.
The animals looked very scared.
These are not my ancestors, thought
Fluffy. **No way!**

WILD
CAVIES

The guide led the class down the hallway.
He stopped in front of a large statue.

Fluffy's eyes got very big.
Yes! he thought. **Here is my ancestor!**

Grandpa! thought Fluffy.
I'd know you anywhere!

T-Fluffy

The guide showed Ms. Day's class
all sorts of dinosaur skeletons.
Some were huge.
Others were as small as lizards.
Some had horns.
Others had wings.
Big deal, thought Fluffy.

"No dinosaurs are alive today,"
the guide said.
"Why not?" asked Wade.
"Some scientists think that
millions of years ago,
a comet hit the earth," the guide said.
"It caused terrible dust storms.
The dust blocked out the sun.

Without sunlight, green plants died.
The dinosaurs had nothing to eat.
So they died, too.
Other scientists think flying dinosaurs
may have changed into birds.
But no one knows for sure."
I do! thought Fluffy. **I do!**

After a comet hit the earth,
tour guide Fluffy told his group,
most dinosaurs died. But not T-rexes.
They were too tough to die.

When dust from the comet
blocked the sun,
the Earth got cold. Brrrr!
It was an ice age.
So what did smart T-rexes do?
They grew fur coats!
Furry T-rexes survived the ice age.

For some reason, guide Fluffy went on,
fur never grew very well on T-rex tails.
So their tails froze and dropped off.
But who needs a tail?

Now, if there was one thing a T-rex loved,
it was a big, juicy carrot.
Luckily, carrots survived the ice age
because they grew underground.
T-rexes got down on all fours
and dug up carrots all day long.
Pretty soon T-rexes forgot that they ever
ran around on their two back legs.
T-rexes became four-legged creatures.

There was only one problem,
said guide Fluffy.
Big T-rexes had to eat 3 1/2 tons
of carrots every day just to stay alive

It was hard work finding so many carrots.
But small T-rexes had it easy. They could fill up on just a few carrots.
So, over millions of years, T-rexes got smaller and smaller.
They ended up no bigger than grapefruits.
And they looked just like...

...me.

Mice and rats are rodents,

said guide Fluffy.

**But a guinea pig's ancestors
go back to the age of dinosaurs.**

Wade held Fluffy on the bus ride
back to school.

"I wish the dinosaurs were still around,"
he told Maxwell.

"Yeah," said Maxwell. "It would be cool
to have a dinosaur for a class pet."

Yeah, thought T-Fluffy.
Very cool!